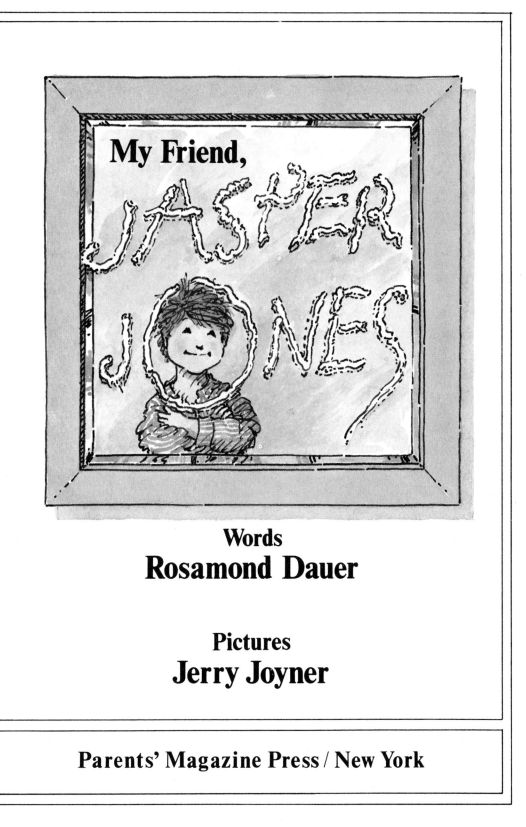

My Friend, JASPER JONES

Words
Rosamond Dauer

Pictures
Jerry Joyner

Parents' Magazine Press / New York

Library of Congress Cataloging in Publication Data
Dauer, Rosamond.
    My friend, Jasper Jones.
    SUMMARY: A child who blames everything on a
    make-believe friend must eventually clean up after him.
I.   Joyner, Jerry.   II.   Title.
PZ7.D2615My   [E]   76-2459
ISBN 0-8193-0887-0   ISBN 0-8193-0888-9 lib. bdg.

For Christian and Brilla Milla

The Beginning

Once, in a nice little town, there was a family that lived in a nice little house. Teddy lived in that nice little house, with his mother and father.

Teddy had a secret friend. His name was Jasper Jones.
No one ever saw him except Teddy. He was make-believe, and
Teddy found him very useful.

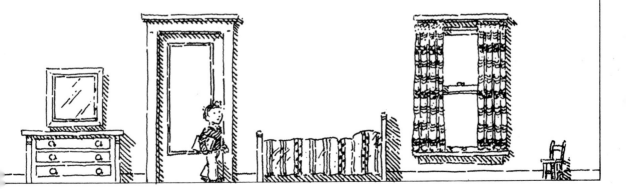

One day when Teddy was not doing very much at all, his bed
broke in his nice little room.

His mother came in and said, "Oh dear, what has happened?"
Teddy, who was sitting in his nice little chair said, "I can't imagine."

His mother looked at him.
Teddy said, "It must have been my friend, Jasper Jones."
"I would like to speak to Jasper Jones," said his mother.

"You can't," said Teddy. "He has gone for a walk."
"I see," said Teddy's mother. "Please give him a message.
NO MORE BROKEN BEDS!"

"I will tell him," said Teddy. "That was not nice of him
to break my bed."

"Indeed not," said his mother.

Teddy's mother and father fixed Teddy's bed by nighttime.

Teddy was glad because his chair was not meant for sleeping.

The Middle

The next afternoon, Teddy was taking a nice little nap
when his father came into his room.

What a surprise! Teddy's clothes were all over the
floor. And his bureau drawers were stuffed with leaves.

There were leaves stuffed in his top drawer.
There were leaves stuffed in his middle drawer.
There were leaves stuffed in his bottom drawer.

Teddy's father asked, *"Now* what has happened?"
Teddy said, "That's a mess, all right. But I didn't do it."
His father looked at him.

Teddy said, "I think it must have been Jasper Jones.
He is my friend. And he is special."
"I would like to speak to Jasper Jones," said Teddy's father.
"You can't," said Teddy. "He has gone for a walk."

"I see," said Teddy's father. "Please give him a message.
NO MORE LEAVES IN YOUR BUREAU!"
"I will tell him," said Teddy. "That was not very nice of
him to put leaves in my bureau."

Teddy, his mother, and his father put Teddy's clothes back
in the bureau. Teddy was glad because his clothes took up
too much room on the floor of his nice little room.

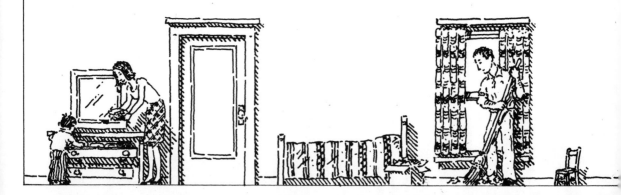

The End

The next evening, after a nice little supper, Teddy played
in his room. He waited for his mother and father.

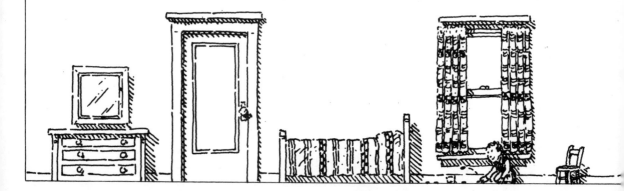

When they came in, they could see that Jasper Jones had been
visiting. One whole wall of Teddy's room had been painted
with peanut butter.

"Not very nice," said Teddy, "is it?"

"No, it is not," said his mother and father.

"But," said his mother, "since Jasper Jones is your friend,
and no one ever sees him except you—"

"That's right," said Teddy.

"And," said his father, "since he has probably taken a walk—"

"Oh yes," said Teddy.

"Then," said his parents together, "you will have to clean up after him."
And they left Teddy all by himself in his room.

So Teddy used buckets of water, and lots of soap,
and washed off his wall. He didn't like having to clean up
after Jasper Jones.
By then, he was very tired, and it was time for bed.

Teddy got into his nice little bed.

His mother and father came to tuck him in.

His mother gave Teddy a hug. His father gave him a kiss.

"Tomorrow," said Teddy, after a nice big yawn, "my friend,

Jasper Jones is going to visit another little boy in another little town."
And that was how Teddy said good-bye to his friend. But he
never forgot Jasper Jones, who was, after all, very special
and nice, in his own little way.

A poet as well as the author of two previous picture books, *Rosamond Dauer* lives with her husband and family in Ridgefield, Connecticut. One of her two sons once had a memorable, imaginary companion named Brilla Milla, whose exploits provided the inspiration for *My Friend, Jasper Jones.*

Jerry Joyner, an illustrator and designer, made his first children's book at the age of five. A former staff member of *Esquire* and Push Pin Studios, he now works as a free-lance artist both in Europe and the United States. He illustrated *How Far Will A Rubber Band Stretch?* for Parents' Magazine Press and collaborated with Remy Charlip on the prize-winning *Thirteen.*